Otto and the Oval bowl

Om KIDZ

An imprint of Om Books International

Om Kidz | Om Books International

Reprinted in 2023

Corporate & Editorial Office
A-12, Sector 64, Noida 201 301
Uttar Pradesh, India
Phone: +91 120 477 4100
Email: editorial@ombooks.com
Website: www.ombooksinternational.com

Sales Office
107, Ansari Road, Darya Ganj
New Delhi 110 002, India
Phone: +91 11 4000 9000
Email: sales@ombooks.com
Website: www.ombooks.com

ISBN: 978-93-52760-31-2

Printed in India

10 9 8 7 6 5 4 3 2

Otto and the Oval bowl

Paste your photograph here

My name is

Otto, the **old owl** lives on an **orange** tree. The tree is **opposite** an **open** well.

Otto loves things to be in **order.**

He always **obeys** rules.

Otto has an **oval** bowl.
This bowl is made **of** wood.
He has made it **on** his **own.**

Only Otto uses the bowl. He does not allow anyone else to use it.

Otto stores **oil** in the bowl.

Sometimes, he keeps **onion or other** vegetables in it.

When the bowl is empty,

Otto keeps it **on** the **oven.**

The **oval** bowl is very dear to **Otto.**

One day, he goes **out.**
When he comes back,
his **oval** bowl is missing.
Otto decides to look for it.

An **ox** is passing by the **orange** tree.
The **old owl** calls him **over.**

"Did you see my **oval** bowl?"

he asks the **ox.**

The **ox** thinks **over** it for a while. Then he says, “I saw the **ostrich** and her baby walking with it.”

The **ox** and the **owl** go to the **ostrich.**

"My baby was thirsty. I used your bowl to pull water **out of** the well," says Mama **ostrich.**

The baby **ostrich** gives the bowl back to **Otto.** **Otto** looks angry.

A big tear comes **out of** the baby **ostrich's** eye. The baby is scared. **"Oh,** we are sorry," says Mama **Ostrich.**

Suddenly, **Otto** the **owl** breaks **out** into a wrinkly smile.

He **opens** his feathers and gives the baby **ostrich** a hug. The **owl,** the **ox** and both the **ostriches** laugh.

Know your words

Naming words

Otto	ox	oven
orange	ostrich	owl
oil	onion	

Describing words

old	oval

Doing words

order	obeys	open

Sight words

of	own	out
on	only	other
or		

Circle all the words beginning with the letter 'O'.

thirsty

onion

order

tear

oven

baby

feathers

oil

Join the dots to find Otto's most favourite object. Decorate it with patterns and colour it.

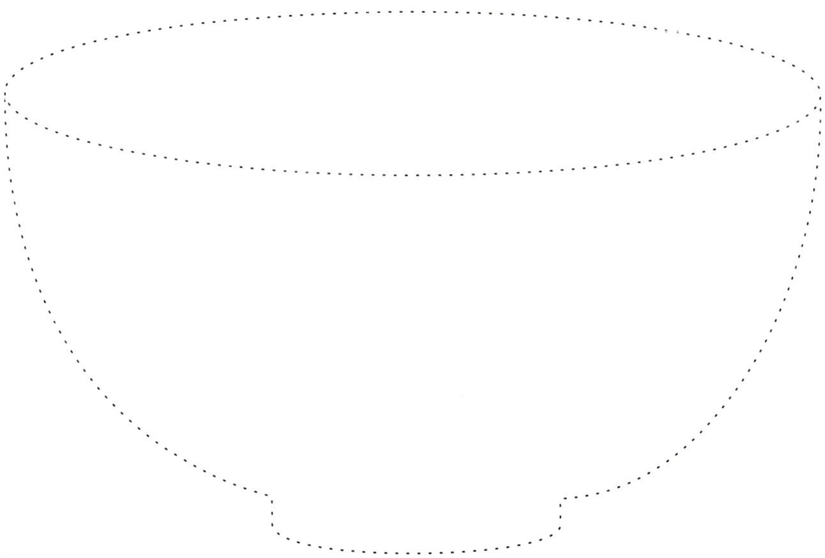

Colour the objects beginning with the letter 'O'.

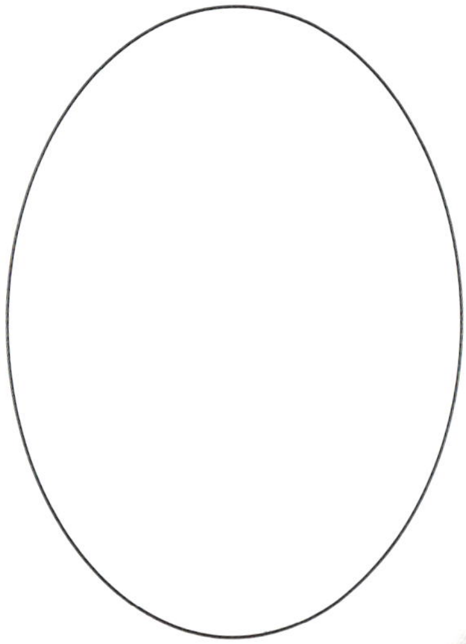